ABOUT THE BANK STREET READY-TO-READ SERIES

Seventy-five years of educational research and innovative teaching have given the Bank Street College of Education the reputation as America's most trusted name in early childhood education.

Because no two children are exactly alike in their development, we have designed the *Bank Street Ready-to-Read* series in three levels to accommodate the individual stages of reading readiness of children ages four through eight.

○ *Level 1:* GETTING READY TO READ—read-alouds for children who are taking their first steps toward reading.

● *Level 2:* READING TOGETHER—for children who are just beginning to read by themselves but may need a little help.

○ *Level 3:* I CAN READ IT MYSELF—for children who can read independently.

Our three levels make it easy to select the books most appropriate for a child's development and enable him or her to grow with the series step by step. The *Bank Street Ready-to-Read* books also overlap and reinforce each other, further encouraging the reading process.

We feel that making reading fun and enjoyable is the single most important thing that you can do to help children become good readers. And we hope you'll be a part of Bank Street's long tradition of learning through sharing.

The Bank Street College of Education

Para Amalia Rosa
—*N.J.*

To Grade Two
—*R.C.*

The author gratefully acknowledges
Professor Ricardo Alegría, the late Pura Belpré,
and the people of Loiza Aldea

SING, LITTLE SACK!
¡CANTA, SAQUITO!

A Bantam Little Rooster Book/June 1993

Little Rooster is a trademark of Bantam Books,
a division of Bantam Doubleday Dell Publishing Group, Inc.

Series graphic design by Alex Jay/Studio J

Special thanks to James A. Levine, Betsy Gould,
Diane Arico, and Melissa Turk.

Library of Congress Cataloging-in-Publication Data

Jaffe, Nina.
Sing, little sack! canta, saquito!:
a folktale from Puerto Rico
/ retold and adapted by Nina Jaffe ; illustrated by Ray Cruz.
p. cm.—(Bank Street ready-to-read)
"A Byron Preiss book."
"A Bantam Little Rooster book."
Summary: Captured and kept inside a sack
by a strange little man, a young girl
is forced to sing, until her mother hears
her song and knows that it is not
the sack that is singing.
ISBN 0-553-09240-5 (hc).—ISBN 0-553-37144-4 (tp)
[1. Folklore—Puerto Rico.] I. Cruz, Ray, ill.
II. Title. III. Series.
PZ8.1.J156Si 1993
398.2—dc20
[E]
92-10743 CIP

Published simultaneously in the United States and Canada

Bantam Books are published by Bantam Books, a division of Bantam Doubleday
Dell Publishing Group, Inc. Its trademark, consisting of the words "Bantam Books"
and the portrayal of a rooster, is Registered in U.S. Patent and Trademark Office
and in other countries. Marca Registrada. Bantam Books, 1540 Broadway, New
York, New York 10036.

PRINTED IN THE UNITED STATES OF AMERICA

0 9 8 7 6 5 4 3 2 1

Bank Street Ready-to-Read™

Sing, Little Sack!
¡Canta, Saquito!
A Folktale from Puerto Rico

Retold and adapted by Nina Jaffe
Illustrated by Ray Cruz

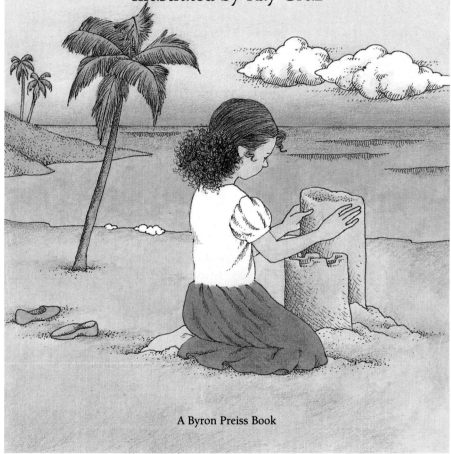

A Byron Preiss Book

A BANTAM LITTLE ROOSTER BOOK
NEW YORK · TORONTO · LONDON · SYDNEY · AUCKLAND

Había una vez y dos son tres . . .
Once upon a time
a little girl named Marisol
lived with her mother
in a small town called Aguadilla
on the island of Puerto Rico.

4

Every night, before she went to sleep,
Marisol cuddled in her mother's arms.
Her mother sang her favorite lullaby:

> *"Duermete, mi niña,*
> *Duermete, mi sol,*
> *Duermete, pedazo de mi corazón.*
>
> "Go to sleep, my daughter,
> Go to sleep, my sun,
> Go to sleep, little corner of my heart."

When Marisol turned seven,
her mother gave her
a special birthday gift—
a pair of golden earrings.

Then she said, "Marisol, today I must
wash clothes in the river.
You may go down to the beach
to play."
"¡Gracias, Mamá!" exclaimed Marisol.
"Thank you!"
And she skipped off into the morning.

Marisol walked through the town square.
She passed *el coquero* selling coconuts.
She passed *los pescadores* casting nets.

She walked on,
down the path,
through the palm trees,
till she came to the beach.

How happy she was!
The sun was shining.
The water was clear and warm.
Marisol took off her new earrings.
She hid them carefully in a tiny hole
in a large rock.

Marisol played all day.
She jumped in the waves and
built tall castles in the sand.

When the sun went down,
Marisol started home.
But on her way up the path,
she stopped.

"My earrings!" she cried.
"My beautiful golden earrings!
I left them hidden in the rock."

It was getting dark.
But Marisol turned around.
She went back down the path to the beach.

There was the rock.
Her earrings were still inside.
But sitting on the rock
was a strange little man.

His eyes were yellow,
and his face was green.
His vest was purple.
His shoes turned up at the toes.

In one hand he carried a great big bag.
In the other he carried a stick.
"Please, sir," said Marisol.
"May I get my earrings?"

"Of course you may," said the little man.
"But first you must sing me a song!"

Marisol was afraid.
But she wanted her earrings back,
so she sang her favorite lullaby:

"*Duermete, mi niña,*
Duermete, mi sol,
Duermete, pedazo de mi corazón."

"I can't hear you,"
said the little man.
"*Acércate.*
Come a little closer."

Marisol took one step closer
and sang again.

"Duermete, mi niña,
Duermete, mi sol,
Duermete, pedazo de mi corazón."

"I still can't hear you!"
said the little man.
"Come closer!"

Marisol took another step closer
and started to sing again.

*"Duermete, mi niña,
Duermete, mi sol—"*

But before she could finish her song,
the little man popped Marisol into his bag.
He tied it up tight with a great big knot.

"*¡Ahora te atrapé!*" said the little man.
"Now I have you!
Wherever I go, I'll tell people
about my magic sack.
My singing sack!

"I'll become famous and rich.
And when I say '*¡Canta, saquito, canta!*'
you must sing your song
or I'll whack you with my stick!"

It was dark inside the sack.
Marisol could hardly see.
Only one little hole in the bag
let in the sunlight.

"How will my mother ever find me?"
Marisol wondered.
She kicked at the bag
as hard as she could,
but there was no escape.
Marisol was trapped.

Each day the little man
took Marisol to another small town.
He stood in the square and said,
"¡Atención damas y caballeros!
Come, people, come!
Come hear my singing sack!"
And then he commanded,
"¡Canta, saquito, canta!
Sing, little sack!"

And from inside the sack
Marisol sang:

"Duermete, mi niña,
Duermete, mi sol,
Duermete, pedazo de mi corazón."

When people heard the singing sack,
they clapped their hands and cheered.
They gave the little man plates of rice,
fried chicken, and ripe mangoes.

But the greedy man
kept almost all the food for himself.
He gave only scraps to Marisol.

One day the little man came
back to the town of Aguadilla.
He stood in the town square.
All of the people gathered round
to hear his singing sack.
El coquero was there.
Los pescadores were there.
And Marisol's mother was there.

Marisol's mother gasped
when she heard the song.
That is no magic sack, she thought.
That is *mi niña*, my Marisol!
I must help her escape.

She went up to the little man and said,
"What a beautiful song!
I would like to cook you a big pot of
chicken stew, but I need water.

"Could you take this empty pot
down to the river and fill it up?"
The little man was so greedy
he dropped the sack
and ran right down to the river.

As soon as he was gone,
Marisol's mother gathered everyone
around the bag.
They untied the great big knot,
and out popped Marisol,
safe and sound!
"*¡Ay, Mamá! Gracias!*" she cried,
giving her mother a big hug.

"I've found you at last," said her mother.
"But now you must run and hide while
we get rid of this wicked little man."
Marisol ran home as fast as she could.

Then the people of Aguadilla
took the bag.
They filled it up with gooey mud
and old coconut shells
and rotten mangoes.

The little man came back from the river.
"Your singing sack is so wonderful,"
said Marisol's mother.
"Why don't you take it to the king?
I'm sure he would love to hear it.
Maybe he will give you a grand feast!"

The greedy little man
forgot all about the chicken stew
and ran right off to the king's palace.
"Your Majesty!" he said.
"Come hear my magic singing sack!"

The king called the queen, his soldiers,
and all of his servants to his throne room
to hear the magic singing sack.

"*¡Canta, saquito, canta!*
Sing, little sack!" said the little man.
The sack said nothing.

So he said again, even louder,
"*¡Canta, saquito, canta!*"
Still the sack said nothing.

"*¡Canta, saquito, canta!*"
he yelled as loud as he could.
"Or I will give you a big whack
with my stick!"
But the sack was silent.

The little man stamped his foot in rage.
He whacked the bag as hard as he could,
and it broke open.
All the gooey mud
and coconut shells
and rotten mangoes burst out.

They fell on the king's throne
and the king's robe
and even on the king's crown!
The king was furious.
"*¡Llevenselo!* Take him away!"

The king's soldiers took the little man
to a cold, dark dungeon.
He slept on the stone floor
and had only scraps to eat.
He was never heard from again.

As for Marisol, the very next day
she went back to the beach
to look for her earrings.

There they were, hidden in the rock
just where she had left them.
"*¡Mis aretes!*" she cried joyfully.
"My earrings!"
She put them on and skipped home.

And that night Marisol
cuddled in her mother's arms.
She went to sleep, as she always did,
while her mother sang:

"*Duermete, mi niña,*
Duermete, mi sol,
Duermete, pedazo de mi corazón!"